# Memoirs of a
# PARROT

### By Devin Scillian and Illustrated by Tim Bowers

Sleeping Bear Press™
2395 South Huron Parkway, Suite 200
Ann Arbor, MI 48104
www.sleepingbearpress.com

Printed and bound in the United States.

10 9 8 7 6 5 4

Library of Congress Cataloging-in-Publication Data

Names: Scillian, Devin, author. | Bowers, Tim, illustrator.
Title: Memoirs of a parrot / written by Devin Scillian ;
illustrated by Tim Bowers.
Description: Ann Arbor, MI : Sleeping Bear Press, [2016] | Summary:
"Join a brilliant, but stubborn, parrot as he endures the banality of the
pet store before being purchased by an equally insufferable young man.
But while things between parrot and owner get off to a rocky start, the
delights of having a pet (or human) bring them both around in the end"
–Provided by the publisher.
Identifiers: LCCN 2015027725 | ISBN 9781585369621
Subjects: | CYAC: Parrots–Fiction. | Friendship–Fiction.
Classification: LCC PZ7.S41269 Mfm 2016 | DDC [E]–dc23
LC record available at http://lccn.loc.gov/2015027725

## A Note on Parrots from In Defense Of Animals International

Parrots can be entertaining and beautiful to look at. They are smart, can learn tricks, and may provide companionship to some people. Unfortunately, the companion parrot has joined the ranks alongside the most discarded, homeless pets in America.

Parrots are inherently wild. Even if captive bred, they possess the same wild traits as their wild born cousins who live in the jungles and rainforests. The parrots' loud vocalizations help them communicate with mates and neighboring flocks in the distance. The parrots' beak is designed for constant chewing, i.e. nest building, breaking and opening nuts, foraging for food, and chewing branches.

These wild traits don't usually mesh well in people's homes or even in outside aviaries. Parrots—the third most popular pet in America— is one of the most frustrating, destructive, messy, and noisy pets a person can have, increasing the odds that the birds will be abused and neglected, and rehomed.

Parrots are highly intelligent and hypersensitive emotionally and physically. Improper handling can teach an already fearful or aggressive bird, or even a tame and loving bird, to bite and become aggressive. These birds require an extraordinary amount of care and attention and can have lifespans comparable to humans.

Millions of unwanted parrots are listed for sale on the internet, in newspapers, in magazines, and are sold at bird marts across the nation. In spite of this, breeders are not slowing down. In fact, millions of baby parrots are flooded into the market every year.

## What Can you Do?

- Adopt and rescue. Never breed or buy birds.

- Report abuse to your local law enforcement when you see it.

- Encourage pet stores to Get Real. Ask them to provide information to their consumers about the reality of keeping parrots as pets.

- Write to your legislators and encourage them to create stronger laws to protect parrots in captivity and to end parrot exploitation.

- Create compassionate, no breed, bird clubs.

For more information visit: www.idausa.org

To my cherished friend Roger Wallace, the only guy
who reads my books as often as I do.
—Devin

To the fond memories of my grandpa and his
African grey parrot, named Chico.
—Tim

## Day One

Wilbur's Pet Shop is closed today.

Good.

No rude people staring into my cage.

I just sit and chat with Tik Tok. We're the only parrots here and apparently the only talkers.

The dogs just yap all day.

The fish don't even try to say anything.

I think the cats might be able to talk.

But they never do.

## Day Two

Wilbur's Pet Shop is open today.

Bad.

The place is packed. Lots of strange people,
and they're all talkers.

> They seem to think my name is Polly
> and that I want a cracker.

> > Uh, no and no.

## Day Three

What is with these people?
They keep asking, "Polly want a cracker?"
That is terrible grammar, by the way.
Tik Tok says I should just try to enjoy the attention.
Please. I'd rather gargle a pinecone.

## Day Four

I'm exhausted.

Today a guy spent an hour asking me my name.

I kept telling him.

"Brock," I said. "Brock! Brock! BROCK!"

He looked very disappointed.

I guess he wanted it to be something else.

Like Polly.

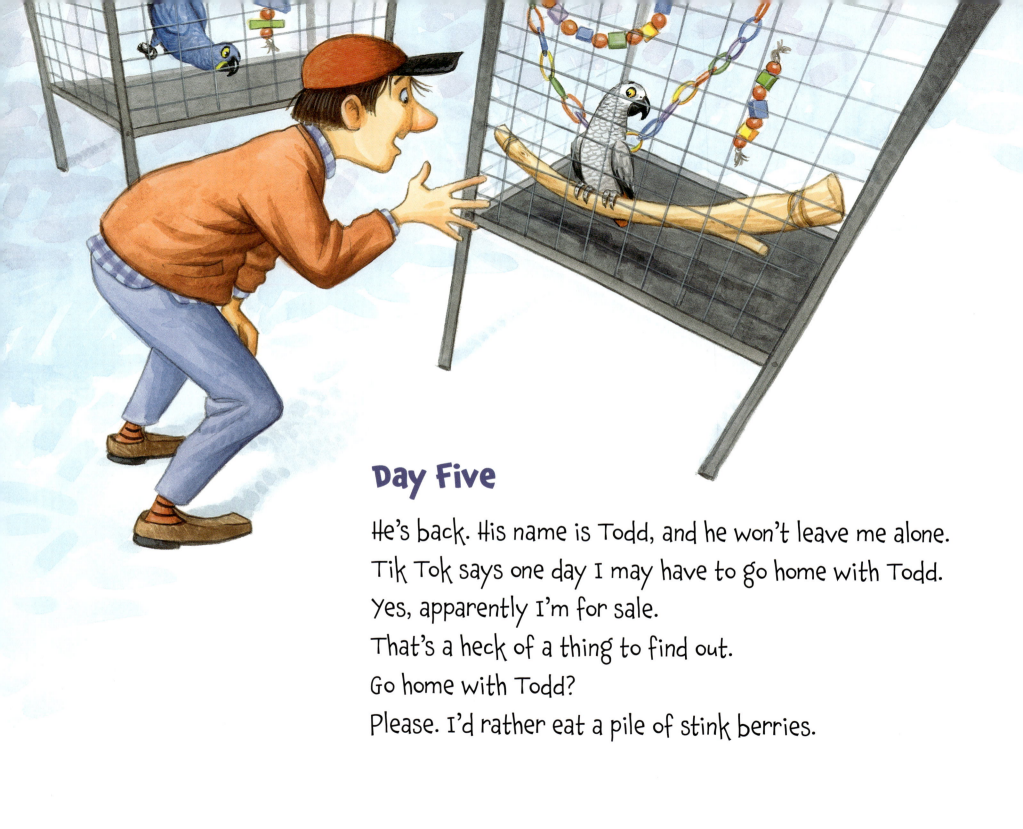

## Day Five

He's back. His name is Todd, and he won't leave me alone.

Tik Tok says one day I may have to go home with Todd.

Yes, apparently I'm for sale.

That's a heck of a thing to find out.

Go home with Todd?

Please. I'd rather eat a pile of stink berries.

## Day Six

Tik Tok was right. Todd handed Wilbur some money
and is taking me home.
This is terrible.
Tik Tok says I need to keep an open mind and that
it could be very nice. Maybe Todd lives in a beautiful
rain forest with lots of bananas and butterflies.
So that could be cool.

## Day Seven

Nope. Todd lives in a tiny house near a freeway. No bananas.

No butterflies. And guess what he does first?

He gives me a cracker.

Seriously?

Even worse, Todd is learning to play the ukulele.

He sounds horrible.

Do I have to stay here?

Please. I'd rather kiss a rattlesnake.

## Day Eight

Todd gave me another cracker today. And just as I was about to throw it back at him, I realized there's a toaster right next to my cage. When Todd wasn't looking, I dropped the cracker into the toaster and then snatched it out of midair when it popped back up. These things are actually pretty good when they're warm.

## Day Nine

Todd came in today with another cracker.

He said, "Say thank you."

So I did.

"Croop!" I said.

"No," he said very slowly. "Thaaaaank yooooouuuuu."

So THAT'S it!

He wants me to speak **his** language. Fat chance.

"Croop," I said.

He sighed and sat down to play his ukulele.

## Day Ten

Here we go again. Todd has his language, and I have mine. Only, it's worse now, because he's decided my name is Echo.

"Echo?" he says.

"Brock," I say.

"Echo?"

"Brock."

"ECHO?"

"BROCK!"

This goes on for hours.

Dude, give it up.

## Day Eleven

Today Todd took me back to the pet shop.

While he complained about me to Wilbur,

I complained about him to Tik Tok.

"It's awful," I said. "He won't even learn my name."

"But you've got a nice cage?" asked Tik Tok.

"Yes, very nice," I said.

"And he keeps you warm and dry?"

"Yep," I said. "Warm and dry."

"And he feeds you?"

"Um, yes," I said. "Toasted crackers. Some figs. Pretty good."

Tik Tok said, "He sounds nice. Maybe he's just not that bright.

He can still be your friend."

Please. I'd rather wear a sweater made of ants.

## Day Twelve

So get this. After two hours of Todd's English lessons, he said, "Echo, maybe you're just not that bright."

**WHAT???**

Not that bright?

I speak seventeen languages!

I can name all the moons of Jupiter.

I can count to a zillion backward! Twice.

Todd said, "It's okay, Echo. You can still be my friend."

Keep your fingers away from my beak, pal. That's all I can say.

## Day Thirteen

Todd gave up pretty quickly today.
It's pretty frustrating. He's learning his
ukulele, but he doesn't really want to
learn his parrot.
His loss. I'm not saying anything.
My beak is sealed.

## Day Fourteen

I'm sitting here, eating a fig and listening to Todd play.

He's actually getting pretty good.

I know, I know—music and figs. How can I complain?

But Todd either needs to learn to talk like me or he can take me right back to Wilbur.

I could explain this to him, but please.

I'd rather set my feathers on fire.

## Day Fifteen

Good heavens, I nearly set my feathers on fire.

Today changes everything.
Todd went to bed last night and I decided to toast a cracker.
I waited for it to pop up.
And waited.
And waited.
But it never did.
Suddenly a lot of smoke started pouring out of the toaster.
There was no keeping quiet any longer.
**"Todd! Todd! TODD!"** I hollered. He woke up, smelled
the smoke, and just ran out of the house!

**Sure, save yourself!** I thought.

The toaster just kept belching smoke into my cage.
Suddenly, Todd came running back into the kitchen.
I thought he was coming back for his ukulele.
But I was wrong.
He came back for me.
Todd reached right into the smoke and unplugged the toaster.
He grabbed my cage, took me outside, and started fanning fresh air at my face.

He'd saved me. I couldn't believe it, but he'd saved me.
He pulled me out of the cage and said, "Echo, are you okay?
Are you? Are you okay?"

What else could I do?
"Thank you," I said.

He looked at me and leaned closer.

"What?"

"Echo says 'thank you'," I said.

Tears welled up in his eyes, and a huge smile took over his sweet, goofy face.

"You're welcome! You're so very welcome!" he cried.

Then Todd said, "You're smarter than I thought."

I said, "You're a **LOT** smarter than I thought!"

He wiped the soot off my face. That was nice.

He sat me on his shoulder, and we watched the moon come up while we waited for the smoke to clear.

Things are different for Todd and me. He's still playing that ukulele. But now he plays and I sing—in his language. And that's okay. He can still be my friend. My best friend. Todd and me? We're staying together. For keeps. Please. There's nothing I'd rather do.